D0601719

With Love, Grandma XOXO

Written by Helen Foster James

and Illustrated by Petra Brown

GMA 1

May 15th

Dear Sweet Pea,

I've always loved letters and hope you will too.

I'm writing this letter in a meadow full of flowers.

If "April showers bring May flowers," it must have been rainy here in April.

You can plant this package of wildflower seeds and watch them sprout.

Grandma misses you, but your love grows in my heart.

I L.O.V.E Y.O.U!!!

With Love,
Grandma
XOXO

Wildflower Mix

May 18th

Dear Sunshine,

I hiked in the mountains today with friends. I took this photo
of a deer and her fawn before they scampered away.
Let's go for a hike the next time you visit CAMP GRANDMA.
Remember how we use our five senses when we hike?
I love you "over the river and through the woods"
and to the tippy-tip-top of the highest mountain.

You'll always be my sunshine.

With Love,
Grandma
XOXO

May 20th

Choo, choo, chug-a-chug-chug!

I hope you like this postcard of the old-timey train I saw today.

Remember our train ride on Chester Choo Choo?

Toot! Toot! Tootsie!

With Love,
Grandma
XOXO

THE GREAT BEAR

May 24th

Dear Doodlebug,

I took a painting lesson outside today.

It's called plein air. That means "open air" in French.

How's that for fancy?!?

I had so much fun, I bought you some paints.

We'll paint together at CAMP GRANDMA.
Let's walk to the park and paint whatever we see.
I hope your day is as pretty as a picture.

With Love,
Grandma
XOXO

May 26th

Dear Precious,

Today I saw a parade with bands playing,

marchers marching,

and flags flying.

I was inspired to write you this rhyme
with some special advice just for you:

Hold on to your dreams
and let your hopes fly.
Look and discover,
be brave, and just try.

I love you and I'm so proud of you.

With Love,
Grandma
XOXO

Knock, knock.
WHO'S THERE?
Orange!
ORANGE WHO?
Orange you going to open the door?

June 1st

Dear Little June Bug,

Today is the first day of June.

Rabbit, Rabbit!

Did you know saying "Rabbit, Rabbit" when you wake up on the first day of a month will give you good luck that month?

Remember telling knock-knock jokes at CAMP GRANDMA and laughing so much?

Keep on laughing and have a lucky month.

With Love,
Grandma

XOXO

June 3rd

Ahoy, Matey!

How's my favorite explorer?

Today I went kayaking, and it was a great, big, full-of-fun day.

We need to plan some more swashbuckling adventures.

I made this pirate's hat for you.

I'll show you how to make one when you visit CAMP GRANDMA.

Wherever our adventures take us,

I'll always love you to the stars and back.

With Love,
Grandma
XOXO

PS Explore more!

June 6th

Hello My Favorite Little Reader,

I found a super bookstore today.

I bought some books for us to read together when you visit.

They say books are gifts you can open again and again.

Remember to remember: the more you read, the better reader you'll be.

You're brilliant and beautiful. I like to say you take after ME! Ha Ha!

Be Sweet, Parakeet!

With Love,
Grandma
XOXO

June 8th

Dear Cutie Patootie,

Remember when we made cards?

They were so glittery and pretty.

You are clever and creative.

Roses are red. Violets are blue.

I love you, Dooby-Dooooby-Doo!

Smile, sparkle, and shine!

With Love,
Grandma
XOXO

June 10th

Dear Snickerdoodle,

I was at the beach today.

The ocean reminded me of this tongue twister:

She sells seashells down by the seashore.

We made s'mores at the campfire this evening.
Do you remember when we made ooey-gooey s'mores
with graham crackers, chocolate, and marshmallows?
They were so yummy, everyone said,
"I want s'more."

Here's a funny saying, but it's true.
"Every day, I LOVE you s'more!"

PS Let's make s'mores when
you come to CAMP GRANDMA!

June 12th

Dear Tootsie-Wootsie!

Splishy, splish, splash!

Drippity-drip-drop!

It's raining today.

Remember how we like to splash about in rain puddles?

We always know how to have fun in rain or sunshine.

See you later, alligator.

Bye bye, butterfly.

With Love,
Grandma
XOXO

June 15th

Dear Cupcake!

My great, big, excellent adventure is over,

and I'm happy to be home.

I hope you'll come visit me soon as you can.

Some people say grandmas are mommies with frosting.

Isn't that funny?

I think we go together like frosting on a cupcake,

and you know how much we both love cupcakes.

Let's have cupcakes and ice cream when you visit CAMP GRANDMA.

I scream, you scream,

we all scream for ice cream.

With Love,

Grandma

XOXO

PS Grandma loves you!

Welcome to
CAMP GRANDMA!

How to Make S'mores

How to Make a Pirate Hat

For Bob

-Helen

♥

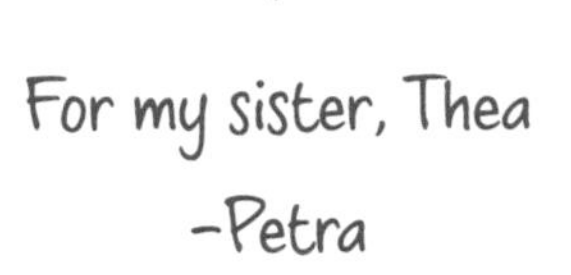

For my sister, Thea

-Petra

Sleeping Bear Press™
2395 South Huron Parkway, Suite 200
Ann Arbor, MI 48104
www.sleepingbearpress.com

Printed and bound in the United States.

10 9 8 7 6 5 4 3 2 1

Library of Congress Cataloging-in-Publication Data

Names: James, Helen Foster, 1951– author. | Brown, Petra, illustrator.
Title: With love, Grandma / written by Helen Foster James ; illustrated by Petra Brown.
Description: Ann Arbor, MI : Sleeping Bear Press, [2018] | Summary:
A grandmother shares her adventures and special memories with her grandchild through a series of letters written while she is traveling the world.
Identifiers: LCCN 2018014170 | ISBN 9781585369423
Subjects: | CYAC: Voyages and travels–Fiction. | Grandmothers–Fiction. | Letters–Fiction.
Classification: LCC PZ7.J154115 Wit 2018 | DDC [E]–dc23
LC record available at https://lccn.loc.gov/2018014170